Jack and Jill

Lucy Cavendish is a journalist, author and a founder member of the Contemporary Women Writers' Club. Over the years, she has written for many publications such as the *Sunday Telegraph* and the *Daily Telegraph*, the *Observer* and the *Daily Mail*. She writes a column about her life in the country with her four children in *Stella Magazine*, part of the *Sunday Telegraph*.

She has also contributed to two collections of short stories, *The Leap Year* and *Ten Past Eight* (available from www.queenbee.co.uk). Lucy has also written three novels for Penguin, the latest of which is *A Storm in a Teacup*.

She lives with her family and many animals in Oxfordshire.

Jack and Jill

Lucy Cavendish

PENGUIN BOOKS

PENGUIN BOOKS

Published by the Penguin Group
Penguin Books Ltd, 80 Strand, London WC2R 0RL, England
Penguin Group (USA) Inc., 375 Hudson Street, New York, New York 10014, USA
Penguin Group (Canada), 90 Eglinton Avenue East, Suite 700, Toronto, Ontario, Canada M4P 2Y3
(a division of Pearson Penguin Canada Inc.)
Penguin Ireland, 25 St Stephen's Green, Dublin 2, Ireland (a division of Penguin Books Ltd)
Penguin Group (Australia), 250 Camberwell Road, Camberwell, Victoria 3124, Australia
(a division of Pearson Australia Group Pty Ltd)
Penguin Books India Pvt Ltd, 11 Community Centre, Panchsheel Park, New Delhi – 110 017, India
Penguin Group (NZ), 67 Apollo Drive, Rosedale, Auckland 0632, New Zealand
(a division of Pearson New Zealand Ltd)
Penguin Books (South Africa) (Pty) Ltd, 24 Sturdee Avenue, Rosebank, Johannesburg 2196, South Africa

Penguin Books Ltd, Registered Offices: 80 Strand, London WC2R 0RL, England

www.penguin.com

First published 2011
1

Set in 12/16 pt Stone Serif
Typeset by Palimpsest Book Production Limited, Falkirk, Stirlingshire
Printed in England by Clays Ltd, St Ives plc

ISBN: 978–0–718–15748–7

www.greenpenguin.co.uk

Mixed Sources
Product group from well-managed
forests and other controlled sources
www.fsc.org Cert no. SA-COC-1592
© 1996 Forest Stewardship Council

Penguin Books is committed to a sustainable future
for our business, our readers and our planet.
The book in your hands is made from paper
certified by the Forest Stewardship Council.

For Ottoline

Chapter One

My mum's face is turning red as she drives me and Jack up the motorway. I can see she's getting stressed out. I know what happens to her face when she gets stressed out. She goes all red and funny-coloured and then the smallest of things sets her off.

Yesterday, it was Jack. Well, it wasn't really Jack. It was his pencil. He couldn't find his pencil but he couldn't tell Mum which pencil it was he couldn't find. I knew which one he wanted, the red one with the rubber on the end, because he gets cross if he can't rub out mistakes. He can't say which one he wanted, of course, because he can't speak, but *I* knew because I always know.

My mum, however, well, she didn't know. All she could see were loads of pencils in his case and they all had rubbers. She kept getting him the wrong one and he did that wordless crying thing he does and she got crosser and crosser and went redder and redder. She was probably going to shout at Jack but then I saw that red pencil. It had rolled under the table, so I went

1

down on my hands and knees and got it for him. Then Jack smiled, one of his wide and happy smiles.

Jack smiles a lot. For a boy who can't speak, he does a lot of other things too, which is how I know what mood he's in. He just has to move his mouth, frown or smile or make this funny grimace he does sometimes, and I know what's going on with him. Sometimes I forget Jack doesn't speak. My mum says it's because I fill his silence with my words, but I don't think that's true. The voice from Jack is his own, not mine.

I don't know why Jack doesn't speak. I can't remember him ever speaking but my mum says he used to. She says when he was a little boy, a baby, he used to gurgle. She says he even said words like 'mama' and 'doggy' but I can't remember him ever doing that. She says by the time he was two, he talked really well.

'People would comment on it,' she says. 'You wouldn't believe it now. They'd say things like, "Doesn't that boy speak well for his age?". He had a lovely voice, pure and high like an angel.' She looks really sad every time she tells me this and it makes me sad too because I'd really like to hear what Jack's voice sounds like. Sometimes I sit and stare at him and try to make myself hear that voice he had. I imagine it in my head, quite

2

a high voice really. I give him words to say like, 'Thank you, Jill' and 'My red pencil please, Jill'. And sometimes, at night when he's getting sleepy and his head has sunk on to his pillow, 'Night night, Jill.' I say 'Night night' back to him.

Sometimes, when my mum's putting us to bed, I see her looking at Jack when it's all dusky and dark and I think she's going to cry. She sits on his bed and strokes his hair as though he's a small boy which, actually, he's not. He's seven now, three years younger than me. Although he's not big for his age, he's strong and wiry. I know that because sometimes, when he gets changed for bed, he looks at me and flexes his arms like he's pretending to be a muscle man. It makes me laugh.

'Strong boy,' I say to him and he giggles silently along with me.

But in the dark of the night with the breeze blowing in through the window, my mum has tears in her eyes.

'Strong boy, Jack,' she'll whisper to him. 'You're my strong boy.'

I think Jack's scared of the night. When the sun goes down and the shadows come into the room he'll sit up straight and look terrified at I never know what. Sometimes I think he's staring at a pile of clothes. Clothes make funny shapes.

Once I saw the outline of a devil's horns in a shirt, another time a wizard's hat in the way Jack's trousers were lying across the chair.

I soothe Jack then.

'It's only a shirt,' I'll say. 'See?' Then I'll tap the shirt up in the air with my foot so it'll land in a different shape and Jack will stop being afraid.

I love the night though. I love the way it cloaks everything and makes it all smooth. Everything outside looks different in the night. Nicer really.

My mum's sighing now. My mum sighs a lot, especially on this journey. She doesn't really like driving. She tells me that all the time. 'Thank God we live in London,' she says. 'You don't have to drive in London.' But I don't think she needs to drive anyway because we never go anywhere.

I think we used to. In my mind I can remember things from when we didn't live where we live now. We used to live somewhere overlooking a park or something like a park. I can remember trees, grass, lots of it. Now and again I'll see something and it's as if I've seen it before. I ask my mum about this. I tell her I remember my old bed with a pink cover on it when we lived in the other place. My mum goes all shut down and says things like, 'It doesn't matter where we used to live.' Sometimes I can remember I had a different bedroom and we didn't have a downstairs. My mum says you shouldn't rely on your memory, but I like it when I remember things.

I remember going to places not just staying in the place where we lived. We went for a picnic to the river once. I remember my dad trying to throw me in the water and he was laughing and I was crying. That's all I really remember of my dad. I think he had dark hair and his chin was scratchy, but that's about it. There are no photos of him anywhere. Mum says it's because we don't have any of him. All I know is, he left when I was five years old. That's what my mum said. Her eyes go bitter when I ask her about Dad.

'He left us, Jill,' she says in a very curt voice and I know what that voice means. It means, DO NOT ASK ANY MORE ABOUT HIM, so I don't.

We're on our way to Auntie Glenda's and Uncle Paul's. That's what my mum calls them, but they're not really our auntie and uncle. They're some sort of cousin. They live on a farm and Mum said that as she had to work so much over the summer holidays, me and Jack should go down there for a bit.

'You'll like it,' she said one night to encourage us. She was talking to me but, really, I knew she meant it for Jack. He had that panicked look on his face.

'Mum,' I said, 'Jack doesn't want to go.'

'Well you have to go,' she said tightly. 'There's no one here to look after you.' Then she softened a bit. She took my hand. 'You'll love it, Jill, really you will, and Jack will too. There's so much to do there and . . . it'll be good for you. Please, tell this to Jack. Look after him, you know?' She looked at me then, almost pleadingly, so I nodded and told her I'd do my best.

After she turned out the light, I went and sat on Jack's bed. He turned his head away from me so I just lay down on the end of his bed and watched his mobile swing round in the small breeze.

'There'll be bugs,' I said. 'Loads of bugs. It's a farm so there'll be more than just bugs. There might be cows and horses and chickens. You like chickens don't you, Jack?'

Jack sat up then and looked at me. I could tell he was thinking he might not like it but, then again, he might. Then he lay back down and fell asleep just like that.

My mum's borrowed a car from a friend. That's what she said. She doesn't really know how to drive it. She'd crunched the gears all the way through town. Jack kept on looking at me every time she made the crunching noise. He raised his eyebrows at me and I had to smother my giggles because I knew Mum would hate it if I laughed at her. She doesn't have to change gear on the motorway though. We can just glide along past all these junctions. I read them out to Jack.

'Maidenhead,' I say. 'That's junction 8/9, Jack.' Then I tell him Newbury, Swindon, Bath, Bristol.

'Ooh,' I say as we swoop on to the M5. 'Now we're heading off to the sea!' I tell him all the tales I know about Glastonbury. We've done it at school. I think King Arthur had a seat there. I tell Jack about that and about the Knights of the Round Table. I can see my mum looking at me through the rear-view mirror.

'Are you sure it was at Glastonbury?' she says. I tell her I'm not sure. Then I sit in silence and Jack looks sad because he likes it when I talk to him. He hears things, Jack does, and he knows things and, sometimes, I think he knows even more than me.

Chapter Two

I must have fallen asleep because when I wake up I can see that Jack is counting lorries. He's licking his finger and marking them down on the window. I tug his sleeve.

'All right, Jack?' I say, sleepily.

He nods, rather solemnly.

'You want to mark them down in your pad?'

He gives me a puzzled look, then shakes his head.

'Just a thought,' I said. 'Nothing more. I was asleep so . . .'

It's a funny thing, Jack's pad. He writes things down in it, mainly the names of insects. He copies them from the *Guidebook to British Insects*. My mum gave it to him a few years back. It's dog-eared now and falling apart. My mum says the glue on the spine has gone, but Jack loves that book and I don't think he minds about the glue.

Jack knows loads about insects now. He spends hours watching them and drawing them. We have a little space outside the back of our house.

It's not a garden. I've seen people's gardens. They have flowers in them and grass that is short. We don't. Mum says she works too hard to have time to do anything to it. 'Someone's got to pay for this house, let alone the garden,' she says but, anyway, I don't think she's that bothered about the garden. There's a lot of tall grass and some nettles. Jack loves the garden because he can find insects there. Just yesterday he brought in something that looked like a beetle, black with red spots on it.

'What's that?' I said, thinking the beetle looked rather dangerous with its long legs and bright spots.

Jack opened his book and showed me the entry.

'Burnet moth,' it said. 'Totally harmless.' Then it went on to say how it had made itself taste horrible so that if a bird ate it, it would spit it out.

I calmed down then.

'Funny that, isn't it?' I said. 'How some things can look really dangerous when they're not. Do you think things that *are* really dangerous look harmless?'

Jack thought for a while then shook his head.

'Oh,' I said. 'Just wondering, that's all.'

We've come off the motorway now. My mum's

muttering to herself and keeps looking down at a piece of paper.

'I don't know why they moved so far out of London,' she's saying to herself. 'North bloody Devon. It's the sodding back of beyond.' She looks down at the piece of paper and suddenly swings into a right turn. Me and Jack bowl over in the back of the car like skittles.

'Sorry,' she says, making that sigh of hers again. 'We're nearly there. I know it's been a long journey but . . .' then we're driving up a track. The dust is flying off the wheels and coming back in through the window. Jack starts to cough. I stare out of the window. All I can see are endless fields. They're not really green though, like I imagined them to be. They're sort of green but there are patches that are brown and dusty. There are no animals in the fields. I've read books about the countryside. It's supposed to be full of meadows and cows. That's how I've always pictured it. This isn't like that at all. In fact, it's so hot, everything seems to be shimmering in the heat.

'What's happened to the fields, Mum?' I ask her. 'I thought they'd be green.'

'It's hot,' she says. 'Not enough rain, Jill. I heard on the news there might even be a hose-pipe ban.'

'Where are the animals?' I say. 'I thought there were animals in the countryside.'

'I don't know how many animals your aunt and uncle have,' she says. She sounds a bit fed up.

Finally, though, I see some cows.

'Look, Jack,' I say. 'Cows! They do have animals.'

Jack raises his head to look out of the window. He smiles broadly.

'Jack's happy, Mum,' I say. 'He likes cows.'

'Good,' says Mum, sighing again.

Auntie Glenda and Uncle Paul come out of the front door when they hear the car. Auntie Glenda gives us a little wave and Uncle Paul smiles. He wears small rectangle-shaped glasses and has a nice smile, big and wide. My mum stops the car and we get out.

'Sorry we're late,' says Mum in a rush. 'It just took so long and I had to borrow a car and . . .'

'It's all right,' said Auntie Glenda, briefly touching my mother's arm. Then she turns to us. 'Hello, Jill,' she says to me.

'Hello,' I say.

'Do you remember me? I met you when you were very little. You were about five I think and . . .'

'How are you, Jack?' Uncle Paul asks, stepping

in. He puts his hand out and Jack stares at him rather solidly. 'Not one for a handshake? Oh well.' Uncle Paul touches Jack lightly on the shoulder then steps back and turns to my mother. 'Journey all right?'

My mum nods her head. She suddenly looks rather tired.

'You must be hot,' says Auntie Glenda. 'A cup of tea? I find it helps in this weather.'

My mother shakes her head.

'I've got to go. I've got to . . .'

'Not even time for a cup of tea?' says Uncle Paul, opening the boot of the car and reaching in to get our bags.

My mother looks as if she is about to cry.

'No,' she says. 'I have to go. I have to get back. It's important that I . . .'

She turns away from us. I see her shoulders tense as Uncle Paul goes to give her a hug, but he stops at the last moment.

'I'll take the kids in, Glenda, OK?' he says. Auntie Glenda gives him a nod.

Uncle Paul leads us into the house. The front door is big and wooden and creaks as he opens it. Suddenly there is a blast of cool air as Jack and I walk from the bright sunlight into the darkness. At first, I can't see a thing. I blink and blink and finally make out a stone-floored hallway with a grandfather clock in the corner. It is going *tick, tock, tick, tock* very loudly.

'That's a very old clock,' says Uncle Paul. 'It belonged to my grandfather. You have to wind it up with a big key.'

I don't know what to say to that so I just stay silent. I feel Jack's hand reach for mine. I am about to take it and squeeze it because I know that's what he likes when he's feeling nervous, but instead he tugs my arm. I look at him. He points to the corner.

'Oh yes,' I say, 'a cat!'

'That's Mr Parker,' says Uncle Paul, nodding at the ancient ginger cat lying in a basket in the corner. 'He's very old. He was here when we came to the farm and no one told us his name so we call him Mr Parker after his old owner. He used to be a mouser but now . . . well, the cat from the next-door farm comes and chases the mice now. Poor old Mr Parker can't do the job, but we can't get another cat because I don't think he'd like it too much if another cat came in to his space.'

Just then, Auntie Glenda comes into the hall in a shaft of blinding sunlight. I can barely make her out, only as a shadow.

'I'll take the children upstairs,' she says to Uncle Paul. As she moves into the dark cool of the house,

I can see her more clearly. She looks worried. Her brow is all furrowed. She motions for us to follow her up a creaky set of stairs. Every step makes a sound. I turn to look at Jack as we walk up them and Auntie Glenda catches me doing it.

'It's an old house,' she says.

When she gets to the top, she turns to the right.

'This is your bedroom,' she says opening a door. It creaks as she pushes it. 'You don't mind sharing with Jack, do you?' I look into the room, Jack peering out from behind me. It's got a sloping roof and a bed tucked into each side. It's pretty but it smells odd, as if it's been unused for quite a long time.

As if she reads my thoughts, Auntie Glenda goes and opens the window.

'It's been locked for a while,' she says, 'but I'm sure it'll be fine with a bit of an airing.'

'It's a lovely room,' I say. 'I share with Jack at home because we've only got two bedrooms so . . .'

Jack squeezes past me. He goes to the bed closest to the window, which has diamond patterns on it and roses outside. He suddenly leans right out.

'Jack!' says Auntie Glenda, panicked. 'Don't do that. You could fall. You could—'

But Jack comes back in. He has a rose in his

hand. He places it carefully on his bed and rummages in his bag and pulls out his insect book. He gives me a questioning look.

'Oh,' I say. 'I bet he's found an insect in those petals. He loves insects you see. He copies them down in to his book.'

Auntie Glenda gives me a look as if to say ARE YOU MAD?

'Right,' she says uncertainly. Jack starts to peel the petals off the rose. 'Well, your mother's gone now. She wanted to say goodbye but . . .'

I look out of the window and see dust rising behind the car as it goes down the driveway.

'Oh,' I say.

'She'll ring. Tonight. So . . . We'll have some tea soon. I was going to cook ham and eggs. Do you like ham and eggs?'

'Yes,' I say. 'Thanks.'

'And does he . . . ?' Auntie Glenda stops for a minute and then whispers loudly to me, 'Does he like that?'

Jack looks at her. His eyes wide. He nods vigorously.

'He's not deaf,' I say to Auntie Glenda. 'He just doesn't speak. That's all.'

Jack is lying on his bed with his eyes closed. We have been in our bedroom for a while now, both silent. Once Jack had dissected his rose – he found one tiny gold-speckled beetle and a small fly and we looked them both up in his guide book – we both agreed we'd take a rest.

'Tired, Jack?' I'd asked and he'd nodded, so we lay on our beds with the window open a bit and let ourselves doze. I could see the sunlight moving over Jack's bare legs. Every so often, the rose bush trembled in the breeze and made a spotty pattern on them. I lay and listened to the slow buzzing of the bees. They have such a constant hum, bees. Buzz. Buzz. Buzzy. Buzz. I felt my eyes closing. The sunlight crept up to Jack's knees. I glanced over at him. He was asleep, mouth open. His insect pad had fallen on the floor. A fly came into the room and zoomed about, hitting the walls and the window pane. Flies must have really hard heads. They bash into everything but never conk out.

Just then, I heard the front door open. The whole house rocked as the door thudded shut. Then I heard heavy footsteps going along the stone floor of the hall. I decided it must be Uncle Paul. I heard him give a big sigh as he moved through the house.

'Glenda?' he said. My aunt came in to the hall-way. 'They OK?' he asked.

'Yes,' she said. 'Tired I think.'

'Poor kids,' he said.

'Yes,' she said. 'It's a lot for them to deal with but . . .'

'That's not what I'm talking about,' he said.

'Yes, I know,' she said, 'but quiet now. It's nearly time for their tea. I want them to be rested. I've made them ham and eggs. They said they liked that.'

'You mean she did.'

'Yes, she did.'

'Terrible what's happened to that boy. Just terrible. I mean, what do you think he—'

'Stop it, Paul,' Glenda said sharply. 'Now is not the time. I'm going upstairs to get them up, so mind your words.'

I heard the creaking of the stairs as Auntie Glenda climbed up to our floor. I lay back quickly on my bed. I didn't want her thinking I'd been listening.

My mum hates it when I listen to her. She calls it earwigging. I try not to let her know I'm listening to her but often, somehow, she knows. Just the other night I heard her talking on the telephone. I don't know who she was talking to but she was saying that me and Jack were leaving the next day.

'To the farm,' my mum said. 'Yes, I do think

17

it's a good idea.' She paused and I thought the conversation was over although I hadn't heard her put the receiver down. But then it started up again.

'Of course that's why they've got to go. I have no choice. No one will know about anything there. It will be a safe place for them. I can't possibly let them stay here and for people to realise . . . I don't know what else to do.' Then she said, 'Yes, I know. I know. I think it'll be OK.' Finally she hung up and sighed. I felt really sorry for her because I could tell by her voice she was sad. I would've gone and given her a big hug but I was supposed to be asleep, so I went back to bed. I spent half the night wondering who she had been talking to.

Auntie Glenda knocks softly on the door. I can see Jack stirring.

'Can I come in?' says Auntie Glenda. 'Are you asleep?'

I get up off my bed. I feel sticky and hot. Despite the small breeze, my hair is damp on my forehead. Jack, I notice, has gone a bit pink. I lift the latch on the door and open it. Auntie Glenda is standing there holding two glasses of juice.

'It's fresh,' she says. 'It's from the apples in our orchard.'

I take one from her and go and sit on Jack's bed. Auntie Glenda hovers behind me.

'Jack,' I say gently. I lean over him and touch his forehead with my fingers. 'Jack, it's time to wake up. It's tea time and Auntie Glenda's brought you a lovely fresh juice.'

Jack starts to move slightly from side to side. It's the only thing about him that bothers me, his silent waking. He doesn't even grunt. I usually make a joke of it. I tell him all the girls will love him when he's older because he'll never snore. Mum tuts disapprovingly at me when I say this.

Jack moves a bit more. His eyes open. He looks all unfocused and fuzzy.

'Here,' I say. 'Sit up and drink.'

I take a long sip. The juice is delicious. It is cool and sweet all at the same time and it's more appley than any apple I've ever tasted. Jack sits up and takes a huge gulp. He closes his eyes.

'He likes it,' I say to Auntie Glenda. 'It's really lovely.'

Auntie Glenda blushes a bit.

'Your Uncle Paul's in now,' she says, 'and it's time for tea.'

Chapter Three

I can't remember going to sleep in my bed on the farm. I must have been really tired because one minute I remember Auntie Glenda kissing me goodnight and the next I was woken up by the sound of a cockerel crowing. I lay in bed and listened to it. It was going *cock-a-doodle-doo* just like they do in this book Mum used to read me. I still have it, pushed back under my bed at home. I found it the other day when I was looking for my favourite hairband, the one with a really big rose on it my mum got me for Christmas last year.

I love hairbands but I don't have very many. My friend Shanice from school has got loads of them. One day her mum asked my mum if I could go and play at Shanice's house, but my mum said no. I cried on the way home because I really wanted to see the hairbands. When I told Mum that, she just went to the shop and bought me some more for my hair, but it didn't stop me crying.

Jack hates it when I cry. I can tell he does

because he looks as if *he* is going to cry and it's really difficult for him because he can't make any noise. I've tried it myself, to see what it felt like. I told Jack to stamp on my hand as hard as he could, but he shook his head and refused. I got so cross, I ended up shouting at him. I said, 'Stamp on my hand, you stupid boy!' I could tell he was getting angry. Then, all of a sudden, he reached out and pulled my hair, and it really hurt. I started to cry really loudly. Then I remembered I was supposed to be silent like Jack so I tried to stop making any noise, and it was really difficult.

That cockerel is still at it, just like the one in the book I got from under the bed. The story was about a dog who snored all night. All the farm animals tried to wake him up by mooing or grunting at him, but it was only when the cock crowed good morning that the dog woke up. He was very happy, but the other farm animals were so exhausted they went to sleep.

My mum thinks I pretend to lose things because I'm nosy. She says I shouldn't be as nosy as I am. I don't think I'm that nosy. I just like to know what's going on. I tell my mum we should have a television and then we'd know what's going on. She just says things like 'we can't afford it' and 'everything on television is rubbish', but

I don't believe her. Shanice says her dad told her you can pick up TVs really cheaply these days, but my mum's funny about things like that. Once I was looking for some glue in the desk drawer downstairs and my mum had a fit when she came in and found me there.

She said, 'What are you doing in that drawer? Get out of there now,' just like that. She shouted so loudly that it scared me. Jack was in the room, drawing in his book or something. He ran to the sofa and put his fingers in his ears and rocked backwards and forwards, which he only does when he's really frightened.

'I was only looking for some glue,' I said. 'I was making a picture of a butterfly and I wanted to stick some sparkles on it.' I thought I was going to cry then because I really *was* making a picture of a butterfly. Mum came to me and pulled me to her really roughly. She took me over to the sofa and we both sat near Jack and she stroked his head until he took his fingers out of his ears.

'Sorry,' she said. 'It's just I keep telling you, Jill. If you keep on looking for things, well . . . it's not good. That's my drawer. It's an adult drawer. Sometimes you've just got to keep out.'

It's not like that here on the farm though. It's all open and wide. I go and sit on the end of Jack's bed and stare out. I can see the farmyard with the chickens clucking round it. They look so busy pecking with their bottoms going up and down. Beyond the farmyard is just fields, huge fields. I've never seen anything like it. I look across at Jack. He's still asleep, although I have no idea how he can be because the sun is pouring through the window on to his face.

At breakfast, Uncle Paul tells us he's going to take us to the cow sheds after lunch.

'Have you got old clothes on?' he asks, peering out over his glasses. 'It's pretty rough in there. Those cows don't take any prisoners.'

'Paul,' Auntie Glenda says sharply.

'What?' says Uncle Paul. He winks at me and Jack. 'It's true. They have to be fed, Glenda. The grass is all dried up and those cows jostle. You know that. I'm just warning them' – and he nods towards us – 'so they don't get knocked over, you know? It's hot and cows don't like the heat. It makes them tetchy.'

Auntie Glenda purses her lips and pours him a cup of tea.

'Toast, children?' she asks us brightly. 'Or crumpets? I've even got some cereal . . . or porridge maybe?' She looks at me expecting an answer.

'I'd like toast and jam,' I say. I look at Jack.

'What would you like, Jack?' I ask him. He points to the crumpets. 'He'll have crumpets,' I say. Jack points to the butter. 'And butter.'

On the way to the cow pens later that day, Jack tugs on Uncle Paul's sleeve.

'What is it, Jack?' Uncle Paul asks him. He bends down towards him, waiting for Jack to do something but Jack doesn't do anything. He just stands stock still and stares into the air.

'You hot?' says Uncle Paul. 'It feels as though the heat's bouncing off the earth. It's a scorcher, isn't it? Mind you, it'll rain later. Can you smell it?'

Jack doesn't do anything. He just stands as still as can be. Uncle Paul looks at him questioningly.

'What is it, Jack?' Uncle Paul says again but then, suddenly, Jack falls down onto his knees and starts crawling through the grass by the side of the path. He's going as fast as he can, legs moving like pistons.

'What's he doing?' Uncle Paul says to me, sounding worried. 'Does he often do this?'

I shake my head. 'Not really,' I say.

Then, just like that, Jack lunges forward, arms outstretched, hands open. He stands up. He has something cupped in his hands. He looks at Uncle Paul expectantly.

'What have you got in there?' Uncle Paul asks him. Jack shrugs his shoulders but his eyes are shining.

He opens his hands slightly as Uncle Paul bends to take a closer look. Suddenly Uncle Paul jumps back and a small green insect leaps from Jack's hand.

'Oh! It's only a grasshopper,' Uncle Paul says laughing. He ruffles Jack's hair. 'Silly me. It just took me by surprise.' Jack looks at him and then takes his insect book out of his pocket.

'What's that?' asks Uncle Paul.

'It's his insect book,' I say. 'Mum gave it to him. He looks everything up in it. He loves insects, you see. He'll probably draw it later. That's how he knows so much about them.'

'You're a funny boy aren't you, Jack?' says Uncle Paul and then he rests his arm lightly on Jack's shoulders. I can tell Jack likes it because he's beaming at me.

When we get to the cow shed there are so many cows mooing and pushing and barging around I can barely make out one from the other.

'THEY'RE VERY NOISY, AREN'T THEY?' I shout to Jack. He nods his head.

'THEY'RE ABOUT TO BE MILKED!' shouts Uncle Paul. 'THAT'S WHY THEY'RE MAKING SO MUCH NOISE.'

I stare at the cows all jostling around. They have twitchy ears and swishing tails and they're covered in flies.

Uncle Paul nods his head for us to follow him and he walks down the length of the big shed and then turns right towards a much smaller pen.

'This is where the calves are,' he tells me as we follow him. 'The female calves we keep for milking and the male ones, well . . .' He stops talking then because we've reached the pen. 'Most of these were born in the spring,' says Uncle Paul. 'That's when most of my cows calve, but you can get some in the autumn . . .' Uncle Paul trails off, then he says, 'They're still only babies really, in their own way.'

Jack and I stop next to the bars and there, standing in front of us, is the most beautiful calf I have ever seen. It looks all soft and buttery and its skin looks as if it's streaked with caramel. It has great big brown eyes and a sweet face and it has planted its two front feet into the ground as if trying to stop itself from coming near us. Its eyes are all goggly and it's making a funny snorting noise.

'I always thought cows were ugly,' I say to Uncle Paul, staring at the calf.

'Why's that?' he asks.

'They have very long faces, don't they? I always think they look a bit serious.'

'Yes,' Uncle Paul says smiling a bit. 'They do. I suppose they are quite odd-looking when you think about it.'

Just then the beautiful calf comes close and leans its head through the bars and starts sniffing Jack. It has a big wet nose. I don't think I'd like it to sniff me very much, but Jack is smiling away. Suddenly, the calf puts out this huge long tongue and licks him.

'Oh, Jack,' says Uncle Paul watching him as Jack doubles over. 'That cow likes you! Isn't that funny?' Jack stands back up and nods, a grin ear to ear. He starts rubbing his hand across the calf's face.

'They've got rough tongues, haven't they?' says Uncle Paul. 'Like sandpaper. Now, you must remember to wash your hands when you get back inside. Animals can carry diseases you know. They might look cute but they can give you all sorts of things you don't want to know about.'

Suddenly there's a noise behind us, a crunch on the gravel and a small beep of a horn.

A van pulls up and a man gets out. He's wearing a cap. He nods towards Uncle Paul and then gets something long and thin from the back of his truck. I can't quite make out what it is.

'What's that?' I say to Uncle Paul.

'Time to go back to the house,' Uncle Paul says quickly. 'I've got to go and see this man about a job.'

He takes Jack by the elbow and starts steering him away from the pen.

'Off you go then, Jack,' he says. 'Go and draw that grasshopper. I'll look at it later, eh?' Uncle Paul gives me a nod.

'All right,' I say and Jack and me start off back past the long shed towards the house.

I turn round to wave goodbye to Uncle Paul. I can see that he and the flat-cap man have caught a calf, not the beautiful one but a different one. They are trying to move it into a pen on its own. Their faces are red because the calf has planted its feet and is refusing to move. Uncle Paul is pulling hard and the other man goes round the back and starts to push. Uncle Paul looks up and sees me and suddenly looks a bit cross and worried, I don't really know why. He waves his hand at me sharply as if to tell me to go away. I don't like the look of what's going on, so I grab Jack by the hand and pull him as fast as I can back towards the farmhouse.

Chapter Four

When we get through the farmhouse door, I can see the sky darkening just at the horizon.

'That's weird,' I say to Jack. 'Do you think Uncle Paul could be right and there is going to be rain?'

'More than that,' says a voice from the corner. 'I reckon there's going to be a great big thunder-storm.'

'Who's that?' I say. I can't see anyone because I've just come in from the outside and my eyes are blinded.

Just then Auntie Glenda comes bustling in to the room.

'Ah,' she says to me, 'Jill. Someone's come round to see you. This is Dick.' She points to the boy who I can now make out is sitting in the corner. 'I thought it would be nice. He's only a year older than you and—'

'Bet you I was the only kid she could think of,' says the boy standing in front of me. He's barely taller than me but he's a bit like Jack, thin but strong-looking. He has lots of brown hair and freckles across his face. He has a funny accent too. To my surprise, Auntie Glenda laughs.

'Oh, Dick dear,' she says. She shoos at him with her duster. 'Dick lives in the farm next door,' she says. 'His dad's just dropped him off.'

'Is your dad the man in the van?' I ask him.

'Yep,' says Dick. 'He's come round to—'

'How about a cool drink?' Auntie Glenda says quickly. 'Maybe even a slice of fruit cake. Dick's mum dropped some off yesterday. She makes lovely home-made cakes, Dick dear, doesn't she?'

I look at Dick. He winks at me. Then he turns back to Auntie Glenda.

'What's happened to your telly?' he says. He says *'appened* not *happened* and *wha'* instead of *what*, which my mum has told me is the wrong way to speak. She says you must pronounce your '*t*'s so it's *night* not *nigh'* and it should be *isn't it* not *innit*. You must say your aitches too, so it's *horses* not *'orses*.

'The television?' says Auntie Glenda. She looks flustered. 'It's broken. I'm going to get your juice and cakes so wait here, OK?'

'Broken?' says Dick almost to himself. Then he says to me, 'I saw that programme just the other day on it. I was round here and it was the one where the kingfisher goes hunting to feed

Mrs Kingfisher and all the kingfisher babies. Did you see it?'

I shake my head. 'We don't have a telly either,' I say.

'Oh,' he says. Then he says, 'That kingfisher went out over 30 times in half a day to get insects. Do you know how many insects over a mating period that means it eats? Hundreds like. Maybe even thousands!'

I catch sight of Jack. He looks horrified.

'What's the matter with you?' Dick says to him, noticing the shocked look on Jack's face.

'He likes insects,' I say.

'Right,' says Dick. Then he looks at me. 'Does he collect them?'

I shake my head. 'No. He looks them up in a book and then copies them down into his pad. He's really good at drawing them actually.'

Dick gives me a funny look.

'Your aunt says he doesn't speak. Is that right?'

I nod my head. 'But I understand him,' I say. 'He's my brother.'

'Don't you really speak?' he asks Jack.

Jack shakes his head.

'Why don't you speak?'

Jack shrugs his shoulders, then looks away from Dick in an uncomfortable fashion. I'm about to tell Dick it really doesn't matter Jack doesn't speak because he speaks to me, when Dick goes over and pats him on the shoulder.

'Don't you worry about it. Sometimes people don't speak much because, most of the time, there's not much to say, is there?'

Jack nods his head enthusiastically.

'I hear people speak all the time,' Dick continues, 'and they're just blathering on. You stick with me and you'll be all right. If it's insects you like, I can show you zillions of them. It's the countryside. We've got nothing much here but insects!'

Auntie Glenda comes back in with a tray. On it is a big jug, some coloured plastic tumblers that look like jewels and some slices of cake. She looks from me to Dick and Jack, and then she looks relieved.

'Right,' she says briskly. 'You lot seem to have sorted it all out. Have a cool glass of elderflower cordial and a slice of cake then go out to play.'

Dick helps himself to the biggest slice of cake.

'Don't go to the cow pens, Dick,' Auntie Glenda says sharply. 'Your dad's there.' She gives Dick a hard look.

'All right,' he says, his mouth full of cake. 'I'll take them somewhere else. We'll go on a bug hunt. Would you like that?' he asks me and Jack.

Jack nods enthusiastically.

'Yes,' I say. 'We would like that.'

A while later, we are walking across a big field towards a grassy bank right at the very bottom of it.

'That's where the insects are,' Dick says. 'They're in the very edges. Farmers have to keep long grass at the edges of the fields now so wildlife can live there. You wouldn't believe what you can find at the margins of a field.'

'Like what?' I ask him.

'I've seen field mice and voles, and once I saw an adder. It was lying so still I nearly didn't see it, but it had good markings on its head like an arrow.'

'An adder?' I say. 'Aren't they poisonous?'

'Yes,' says Dick, 'but, you know, I think they keep themselves to themselves.'

By the time we get to the field I am hot and thirsty. The sun isn't out now because the clouds have come over, but it's still baking hot and I'm all sweaty. My mum says days like this are like being in a sauna. Jack's hair is stuck to his forehead. He has small drops of sweat on his brow.

'You hot, Jack?' I say. He nods, so I go over to him and push his hair back. 'Any better?' Jack nods again.

'What shall we look for?' Dick says.

I shrug my shoulders and sit down. Jack starts pushing his way through the grass and bending down to peer through the fronds.

'Why are you sitting down?' says Dick. 'Your brother's having a good time. What's wrong with you?'

'I'm tired,' I say. Suddenly I feel a bit sad. I don't know what I'm doing out here in the middle of nowhere with this boy I barely know. I lie on my back and look at the sky. The clouds are dark and joined together like mourners at a funeral. 'I don't like the look of those clouds,' I say.

Dick looks up. He sighs. 'We'd better be quick,' he says. 'I don't like the look of them either. If we had longer . . .'

'What?' I say, sitting up and looking at him. 'What if we had longer?'

'I'd take you to the stream. It's only one field down. We could've paddled, but . . .'

Suddenly Jack appears in front of us. In his hands he has something that is buzzing angrily.

I leap up.

'Oh, Jack!' I say. 'What's that? I don't like the sound of it.'

Jack grins and opens his hands a little wider. Whatever he has is buzzing even more and I can

34

see yellow and black stripes through the gaps in his fingers.

'Take it away!' I shout. 'It's a wasp, isn't it? You know how I hate them, and you'll get stung. Let it go, Jack, and stop being stupid!'

I turn to look at Dick but he is just staring at what's in Jack's hands.

'That's amazing,' he says. 'Really amazing. Now, open your hands very slowly and let me see what you've got, because I think you've got . . .'

Jack opens his hands a little more. Dick cranes his neck forwards.

'Yes!' He turns to me. 'Do you know what your brother has in there?'

'No,' I say, 'and I don't want to. It sounds scary. Get him to take it away.'

'You think it's a wasp or a hornet, don't you? But it's not a hornet. It looks like a hornet but it's actually a moth. I don't how he found it in the daytime. Where did you find it?'

Jack nods towards the hedgerow.

'Ah,' says Dick. 'Right, now. Yes, they do like the hedges at the edge of a field. Let it go and we can see it fly.' Jack opens his hands and throws them up to the sky and out it comes, this yellow and black humming thing. Even though Dick has told me it's a moth, it still looks scary to me.

'I want to go home,' I say, watching the hornet moth fly crazily away.

'Back to the farm?' Dick says. I nod. 'All right then,' he says.

As we get nearer to the house, drops of rain the size of eggs start coming down.

'Run, Jack, run!' shouts Dick. He reaches out for Jack's hand and tugs him faster and faster up the lane to the yard and on towards the house.

I am running so fast I think my heart's going to come right out of my chest. Then I feel a big dollop of rain land on my head. It's cold and wet. I look up to the sky. It's so dark, all the clouds have gathered into one big one and they're rolling round like they're in a barrel. 'A storm!' I yell. 'It's a storm.'

We run faster and faster and the drops start coming more quickly now. Plip. Plop. Plip. Plop. Plip-plop-plip-plop. Plip-plop-plip-plop-plip-plop.

'Nearly there,' says Dick. His hair is flattened to his head. I can't tell if Jack is laughing or screaming. His mouth is open and his face is red. He opens his mouth really wide and tips his head up to the sky.

'No time for that,' Dick says, pulling on his hand again. 'That lightning's going to be here soon.' He points towards the field furthest away and there it is suddenly, a big flash of lightning shooting down like a snake's tongue.

Jack stops as if someone put a brake on him. He turns to stare at the lightning.

'It's forked,' says Dick, shouting above the noise of the thunder, 'and it's coming our way. Let's move it.'

But Jack looks as if he can't move. He's just staring at the lightning and I think he's trembling. Dick gives one last huge tug on his arm, and we all set off running our hearts out again.

Finally, we burst in through the door panting and wet.

'That was close!' Dick says excitedly. He doesn't seem to notice that Jack is shaking like a leaf in the wind.

'Yes,' I say. I move to Jack and put my arms round him. 'I thought that lightning was going to catch us.'

'Me too!' says Dick.

'Did you think that, Jack?' I say as he puts his head on my shoulder. Suddenly I see Uncle Paul framed by the open door leading in to the kitchen. He's sitting at the large wooden table with his head in his hands. He looks really tired. Dick's dad is sitting at the table opposite Uncle Paul. He is still wearing his flat cap and he gets up when he sees us.

'Hello, kids,' he says slowly. 'Wet are you? Got caught by that storm?'

We all just nod at him.

He turns to Uncle Paul. 'It'll be all right,' he says. 'You'll see.' Then he comes towards us.

'Going on home now, Dick,' he says, 'before that storm really takes off.'

He opens the door. Some drops of rain flick inside the house

'Say goodbye then,' he says.

'Bye,' says Dick and, as he goes out, he looks suddenly really small. I think that he didn't look that small when we were running. He looked big. It must be adults, I think. It's them that make us look small.

Chapter Five

It's impossible to sleep. Jack wanted the window open because he was still hot. The storm is so fierce and the window keeps banging and all I can see is the flashing of the lightning.

'We don't get many storms like this in London,' I say to Jack, but I don't know why I'm bothering. He isn't even moving. He's lying there so still it's as though he's dead or something. He's all covered up in his white sheet with his head sticking out of one end and his feet out of the other. It took him an age to fall asleep because he was trembling so much. In the end, I calmed him down by telling him a story. I told him the one with the snoring dog. I think he thought it was funny because he snuggled right into me as I told him about the other animals getting so cross. Then, finally, I felt his body go all limp.

I can't help talking to him now, even though I know he can't hear me. I think I'm so used to it, I don't know what else to do. It's also because I've suddenly remembered something. As I look out of the window at the storm, I have a memory of Jack standing at a bedroom window, all lit up by lightning.

'Actually, do you remember watching a storm in London, Jack?' I ask him. 'I think you were standing on a window ledge. You weren't supposed to do that. You were supposed to be in bed, but when I woke up, you were on the ledge staring out across the back garden. I went and got Mum. She said you were screaming, but I can't remember you screaming. I wish I could. Maybe that's why you don't like storms. I don't think you've liked them ever since, have you?'

I turn to look at Jack. His mouth is slightly open.

'You're not listening, are you?' I say. Then suddenly I feel a bit angry with him. Why can't he tell me what's going on in his head?

Jack's face is dark and clouded like the sky. I think he must know loads of things. I don't know why he doesn't want to tell anyone about all the stuff he knows. I've closed the window now so I'm hoping I can get some sleep. I have no idea what time it is but it's very late. It must be. We went to bed hours ago but I still don't feel tired.

I screw my eyes tight shut and try counting sheep. I imagine them jumping over stiles with their silly surprised faces and big fluffy bodies.

Then I imagine them all going over backwards, bottoms first and the thought of it makes me want to giggle. I am on sheep number 20 when I hear the telephone ring.

I can't help myself. I get out of bed and creep onto the landing. I know I'm being nosy, but I want to know who's ringing. Maybe it's Dick's dad. Maybe something's happened to one of the cows. I can't hear anything, just low voices coming from the kitchen. I start inching down the steps. If Auntie Glenda or Uncle Paul suddenly comes out of the door and sees me, I will yawn and rub my eyes and pretend I'm on my way downstairs to get a glass of water.

One of the stairs halfway down makes a creaking noise so I stop. I'm feeling sweaty again and my heart is beating fast. The voices murmur on so I shift further down until I can make out what they are saying.

'Who was on the phone?' I can hear Uncle Paul saying.

'You know who it was,' says Auntie Glenda. She sounds tired, just like Mum when she gets back from work.

'What did she want?'

'To see how the kids were. I told her they were fine.'

'Did you?'

'Yes, Paul, I did. They are fine.'

'That's not the way I'd put it.' I hear Uncle Paul sigh. 'I think we should tell them, Glenda,' he says.

'*Tell* them?' says Glenda. She sounds like a scalded cat.

'Yes,' says Uncle Paul, sounding all serious. 'How long can we keep them in the dark? Everyone knows and she can't keep them here for ever.'

'She can keep them here for the summer,' Auntie Glenda says. 'It'll give her some time to work out what to do next.'

'I know that,' said Uncle Paul. He sounds a bit irritated. 'But that boy doesn't speak for a reason. God knows what happened. Haven't you worked that one out yet?'

'Yes, of course I've worked that out,' says Auntie Glenda, 'but we gave her our word, Paul. They are not our children. This is about her and them and what she has decided is the best way through for everyone. We owe it to her. I gave my solemn promise.'

'Oh, Glenda,' says Uncle Paul. I hear the sound of a chair being scraped back. He is obviously getting up from his seat. I tense, ready to run back upstairs in case the kitchen door is about to open. 'It might be the only way you know.'

'It can't be,' says Auntie Glenda. She sounds as if she is going to cry. 'She's just told me no one knows what the outcome is going to be. She has no idea how long it's even going to go on for. We've got to keep them here and not say a word. It's what she asked us to do.'

'I know, I know,' says Uncle Paul. Then I hear the thud of him sitting down on the chair again.

No one speaks for a while. I am about to go back upstairs when I hear Auntie Glenda say, 'Give it all some time. Let them have a nice summer. OK?'

'OK,' says Uncle Paul and his voice sounds as heavy as lead. His chair scrapes back again and I turn and run up to my bedroom before the kitchen door opens.

Chapter Six

The next morning, the storm is all gone, and I go down to breakfast with Jack. I stare at Uncle Paul as he sits, glasses slipping down his nose, spreading butter on his bread. Auntie Glenda is busy in the kitchen making us some crumpets. Jack is playing a game with his knife and fork, spinning them round on the place mats.

'Uncle Paul,' I say, leaning across the table to pour Jack a cup of sweet apple juice, 'has my mother rung? She said she would, didn't she?'

At the mention of my mother, Uncle Paul looks up.

'Glenda,' he calls out. He sounds rather nervous to me.

'Yes?' she calls back from the kitchen.

'Jill was asking if we've heard from her mother.'

Auntie Glenda walks into the room, puts a plate of crumpets on the table and smooths her hands down her apron.

'Yes, we have heard from your mother,' says Auntie Glenda. 'She rang last night. She said to tell you that everything at home is fine. She's really sorry she can't ring during the day while you and your brother are up, but she's very busy at work.'

'Will we be able to speak to her at the weekend?' I ask.

'Yes, of course,' says Auntie Glenda. 'She wanted me to send you all her love and hugs and kisses.'

Jack takes a fresh crumpet.

'What did you say about us?' I ask.

Auntie Glenda looks at Uncle Paul.

'I told her you were having a great time and that Uncle Paul had taken you out to see the cows. Oh, and I told her about Dick. I said how you and Jack had really hit it off with Dick, that you were all firm friends. She said she was really happy about that.' Auntie Glenda turns and goes back in to the kitchen and Uncle Paul stares down at the tablecloth.

Jack and me don't have any friends. That's what I told Dick yesterday. It was the fourth time we'd seen him in four days and he was showing us some stuff called cuckoo spit. It was all round the bottom of some blades of grass and Jack was touching it as though it was made of gossamer.

Dick said to me, 'Aren't you missing your friends?'

That's when I told him. 'We don't have any friends,' I said.

'I thought London was a big place,' he said. 'I thought it was full of people.'

'It is,' I said, 'but my mum doesn't like us seeing people that much. We used to get invited to people's houses for tea, school friends and that, but Mum always said we couldn't go.'

'Well, how could he,' Dick nodded his head towards Jack, 'how could he go? He can't . . . you know . . .'

I sighed then.

'Yes,' I said, 'I think that was the problem. Anyway, Mum likes us at home. Says she feels safer when we're indoors.'

'Safer?' said Dick thoughtfully.

'Yes. Mum says it's dangerous in London. She says you never know when someone's going to do something bad to you.'

'Bad to you?' Dick sounded confused. 'Why would someone do something bad to you?'

'I don't know.'

Then Dick said, 'People do bad things in the country as well, you know.'

He told me and Jack the story of a man who lived nearby who stole birds' eggs. 'It said in the

46

paper he sold them to people abroad who collect them. It's illegal to steal birds' eggs. He got put in jail.'

I told him that Jack had found an egg the other day. It was on the yard, just near the back door.

'It was all smashed up,' I said. 'Jack got all the pieces, well as many as he could, and he brought them in to show me and Uncle Paul.'

'What colour was it?' asked Dick.

'A blue. Not a blue like the sky. It was paler than that.'

'Did it have any markings on it?'

'Yes. It had sort of brown smudges on it.'

'Hmm,' said Dick. 'Sounds like a blackbird's egg to me. Bet the jackdaws got it. They get loads of eggs round here.'

I thought of how Uncle Paul had put all the bits on the table and had started trying to glue it together. He said he was doing it so Jack could see how the real egg looked. He'd given up in the end because there were just too many pieces.

I told this to Dick and he nodded. 'Eggs are difficult things,' he said.

It is so hot today I can barely breathe. After breakfast, Uncle Paul says he has things to get on with on the farm. Jack and I wander out to the cow field, the one where we went insect hunting. Dick told us yesterday you get dragon-flies flying down by the stream there. He said he'd even seen one turn from a larva into an adult.

'They live as larvae for a long time under the water and then they climb up a reed or some-thing like that and their skin splits and the dragonfly comes out,' he said. 'They have to pump up their wings like tyres.'

By the time we get halfway down the meadow, I've been bitten five times and Jack four. What-ever it is keeps on landing on my legs and then I feel a sharp quick small pain.

'What the bloody hell is biting us?' I ask Jack. I scratch away at my latest bite. I look down at my leg. A red bump is coming up large and angry. Jack quickly reaches in to his back pocket and brings out his notebook. He leafs through until he gets to a page then, quick as a flash, he holds it up to me.

'Horsefly,' I say. 'Is that what these things are?' Jack nods fervently. He points to the cows.

'But they're not horses. You've written down horsefly not cowfly!'

Jack shrugs his shoulders.

'Fine,' I say. 'I'm sure you're right. You usually are.'

We walk towards the stream, but although we walk a long way, the end of the field seems to get further away. The stream shimmers beyond it.

'That's a bloody mirage,' I say. 'Jesus, we've been walking for ages.'

Just then I see a small figure swinging through the field towards us from the opposite gate.

'Dick!' I say.

He raises his hands and waves.

'It's Dick,' I say to Jack. 'Do you think he's been bitten as well?'

By the time he reaches us, I've got six bites.

'What's wrong with you?' he asks. 'I keep seeing you scratch your leg.'

'I've been bitten by something,' I tell him.

'Horseflies,' he says.

Jack looks at me and smiles.

'You win,' I say.

'Haven't you smelt a dead animal before?' Dick asks, swirling his stick in the stream. It makes little crescents of waves that circle round in the water and make a pattern.

'What do you mean?' I say. I have taken my shoes off and am paddling in the water. It's not very deep but it's cold and I like the way it feels on my feet. The bottom of the stream is a bit sludgy though, which I don't like. I keep feeling something soft and muddy in between my toes.

'Do the cows come in here?' I asked Dick when I first went in.

'Why?' he asked.

'Because I can feel something soft on the bottom of the stream and I thought it might be . . .'

'Cow poo?' he says. 'Nah. It's probably weed and silt. That's what's at the bottom of most rivers and streams. Bugs live in it. Bugs that ducks like to eat.'

But then we smelt this horrible smell and I asked Dick what it was and that was when he told me it was a dead animal.

'Go on. Do this,' he says now. He puts his head up in the air, nose first like one of those dogs I've seen in books, and takes in a deep breath.

Yep,' he says. 'Whatever that is, it's dead.'

I copy what he's just done. I tip my nose up and breathe in. The smell is like something gone off in the fridge only worse. I see Jack watching me. He is sitting on a stone and staring. I suddenly get a wave of the horrible smell, like rotting flesh or how I'd imagine rotting flesh to be.

'Yuck,' I say. 'What is it?'

'Like I said,' says Dick. 'It's a dead animal.'

Jack gets up and goes over to the reeds lining the banks of the stream. He starts poking about with a long stick he found on the bank.

'You reckon it's over there?' Dick asks him. Jack nods.

'Probably right,' says Dick. He gets up and joins him. I sit on the tree stump next to the bank and put my feet back in the water. A small fish swims up.

'It's a fish, Dick!' I say. 'It's on my toes.'

Dick isn't listening. He and Jack are standing by the reeds. Jack looks sad.

'Oh dear,' says Dick. 'It's a duck. A dead duck. That's the smell.'

Jack starts poking at the reeds again.

'No. We won't move it. It's half eaten. It'll fall apart if we try to put it somewhere else and then it will really pong. We'll have to leave it and hope the wind changes.'

They both come back over to where I am sitting.

'Don't you know those smells?' Dick asks me. 'I can sniff out a dead animal a mile off, even a shrew or a vole. In fact I once saw a male duck, a drake, trying to . . . to . . . with a dead female duck.'

'Trying to do that?'

'Yes,' says Dick looking away. 'It wasn't very nice.'

I lie back, closing my eyes and letting my feet drop down to the silt. It sifts over my toes.

Suddenly I feel a big splash of water on me. It's so cold, I sit up in shock. Dick is standing in the stream in front of me, grinning.

'Thought you were going to sleep,' he says. He splashes me again. That does it. I get up, bend down and then, with as much force as I can, I splash him back. I look up to see his T-shirt is drenched.

'You . . . ! That's freezing!' he yells. Then we're off. I'm splashing him and he's splashing me. My dress is getting so wet it's clinging to my legs like a bandage. My hair is dripping down my forehead and Dick's T-shirt is almost see-through. But on we go, splashing and laughing and running up and down the stream. Suddenly, just when I think I can't get any wetter, Dick stops and puts his hand up.

'Enough!' he says.

'You started it,' I say. I can feel water running down my back.

Dick takes his T-shirt off and lays it on the tree stump. 'Too wet,' he says. 'Not much point in wearing it at all.'

I just stand there and try to catch my breath.

Just then Dick notices that Jack is quite far down the stream from us. He has moved back to where the dead duck is in the reeds. He is poking around with his stick.

'Leave it, Jack!' Dick calls out sharply. 'I've told you before. Aren't you listening to me?'

Jack stops poking the duck but he doesn't turn around to look at Dick. He just stays where he is and I see his shoulders tense up. They always do that when he's angry or upset about something.

'He just wants to bury it,' I say to Dick, trying to wring the hem of my dress out. 'Usually it's only insects.'

'What?' says Dick.

'Look in his pockets. I bet he's got something in there, like a bumble bee in a matchbox. Once I saw him making a grave for a spider.'

'What's that about then?' says Dick.

'No idea,' I say. 'It really freaks Mum out. She hates it, so now Jack does it a bit secretly. I mean, I know about it, but he hides it from Mum so she doesn't get upset. That's why he doesn't like people to know.'

Dick gives me a funny look.

'He won't be able to leave it alone,' I tell Dick, avoiding looking at him. 'He can't bear it, you see, that the duck is dead and it's still out here. He'll want to give it a farewell ceremony or something.'

'He can't,' says Dick shortly. 'This is the countryside. Things die all the time. That duck's bloody rotten. If he moves it, it'll stink. He'll probably get sick from it and . . .'

But then Dick notices Jack has moved back to the reeds again. The next thing I know Dick flies over there as fast as he can and rips Jack's stick from his hands.

'I told you to stop that,' he shouts at Jack. His mouth is pulled back in anger. 'What's wrong with you? I know you can't speak but you're not bloody deaf as well, are you?'

Jack looks up at Dick in shock. His mouth is stuck in an O. Nothing is moving. I go towards him and Dick as quickly as I can but, by the time I get there, Dick has run off up the bank.

Jack won't look at me when I go to give him a hug.

'Jack,' I say. He pushes me away roughly and heads off back towards the field. He walks so fast I have to follow him home all by myself and I get bitten another four times.

Chapter Seven

The next day at breakfast, I see Dick's head pop up at the window just like a jack-in-the-box. He shoots up and gives me a wave, then disappears back down again. I am about to giggle when his head comes back into view. He puts his finger to his lips and looks towards Auntie Glenda. She's making Jack a special breakfast, fried bacon and eggs – that's his favourite.

Last night when we got home, Jack banged really loudly through the front door right in front of me. He was so bitten and upset that Auntie Glenda and Uncle Paul went out of their way to be nice to him. They did whatever they could to cheer him up. They put lotion on his bites. They gave him proper home-made lemonade to drink with ice cubes shaped like animals in it. Uncle Paul sat with him for ages and read him loads of stories from a big old book. One was set in the North Pole and was about an Eskimo who went fishing through a hole in the snow. Jack really liked that one. He kept on tugging Uncle Paul's shirt to make him read it over again.

In the end, Jack fell asleep on Uncle Paul's lap. Uncle Paul struggled up as though he was trying to move a mountain, and carried Jack upstairs and put him to bed. By the time he came downstairs, Auntie Glenda had made me a hot chocolate. I was sitting on the sofa looking at a magazine about chickens. I'd found *Poultry World* under a pile of telephone directories under the coffee table.

'The Rhode Island Red,' I was reading, 'is an American breed of chicken developed in the early 1900s.'

Uncle Paul sat down in front of me and cleared his throat so I stopped looking at the magazine.

'Jill,' said Uncle Paul rather slowly, 'can you tell me what's up with Jack tonight?'

I glanced back down at the magazine. 'In fact, in the past 20 to 30 years, the Rhode Island Red has been overtaken by very efficient hybrids and there are very few breeders of productive Rhode Island Red left in this country.'

'Jill?' said Uncle Paul. I looked at him.

'No,' I said. Then I looked back down at the magazine. I was sure my face must've been burning up because I felt really hot.

'No, what?' said Uncle Paul. 'You won't tell me what was wrong with Jack or you don't know?'

'I don't know,' I said.

'It is not unknown for some strains of poultry to be barely capable of laying 100 eggs a year. This is very few compared to the good old days when birds routinely laid 250-plus eggs and exceptional ones could lay up to 300 a year.'

Uncle Paul got up. He sighed, gave me a long look and went back into the kitchen. I stopped looking at the magazine.

'I'm going to bed,' I called out and gave a big yawning noise so Auntie Glenda and Uncle Paul could hear me. Then I went upstairs to talk to Jack. He was still sleeping so I lay in my bed and counted the leaves on the tree outside.

This morning I am about to tell Jack about Dick being at the window, when Auntie Glenda bustles over with his plate of eggs and bacon. Jack looks up at her, his eyes shining.

'You eat up now,' says Auntie Glenda smiling back at him.

I look out of the window. Dick's face comes into view again. He beckons to me.

'Come out here,' he mouths. I go to touch Jack on the shoulder but first look at Dick again. He looks at Jack and shakes his head. 'Not him,' he mouths.

I am about to refuse to go out. I'm not going to go and see Dick unless he's going to be nice to Jack. Then Dick puts on the most pleading face I have ever seen. 'Please,' he mouths to me.

'Auntie Glenda,' I say in the nicest voice possible, 'may I go outside now? I've finished my breakfast and I promised Uncle Paul I'd collect the eggs. I thought maybe it was best to do it now.'

Auntie Glenda gives me a vague sort of a look.

'Yes. OK,' she says finally. 'Do you know where the basket is?'

I nod.

'What about Jack?' she says. Then she checks herself. 'Oh, Paul was going to show Jack the combine harvester this morning, wasn't he?'

Jack looks at her. He nods his head enthusiastically.

'Don't you want to see it yourself, Jill?' she asks.

No,' I say. 'I don't think I'm that interested in farm machinery. I'd rather get the eggs.'

She nods her head briskly.

'Well, you get the basket and off you go. Paul can take Jack for the morning because I'm off to the market. Will you be all right for a couple of hours?' she asks me. 'Paul will be in the home field if you need him.'

'I'll be fine,' I tell her.

'Just remember not to touch that electric fence round the pens,' she says.

I go into the pantry. Mr Parker, the old cat, is sitting in the egg basket. He is fast asleep. One raggedy, bitten ear is twitching absent-mindedly.

'Mr Parker,' I whisper, 'you have to get out the basket.'

The cat doesn't stir. I go over and start to tip the basket sideways. Mr Parker opens one greeny-yellow eye and stares at me.

'The basket,' I say to him. 'I need it.'

Eventually, once I have tipped it even further, he gets out with a yawn and a stretch.

I hurry to the door and, looking quickly behind me, scoot round to the side of the house where I last saw Dick. He's nowhere to be seen.

'Dick!' I whisper loudly. I can see through the window into the kitchen. Uncle Paul is sitting at the table with his back to me. Jack is eating his breakfast and occasionally looking up at him.

'Dick!' I say again.

Suddenly, Dick's head appears from round the side of the house.

'Shh!' he says. Then he beckons me to go to him. As I get there, he grabs my arm and whispers, 'We have to go somewhere secret. I've got something to tell you.'

'Where shall we go?' I whisper.

Dick thinks for a bit.

'What's Jack doing today?' he says.

'Going to see the combine harvester with Uncle Paul.'

'Good,' says Dick.

That makes me feel cross.

'Why is that good?' I say. 'You were horrible to Jack yesterday. Now you don't want to include him in our game and—'

Dick takes my hand. 'I'm sorry about that, really I am. When I next see Jack I'm going to say sorry to him, OK? It's just that this is *about* Jack, that's why he can't come,' then he starts pulling me along behind the house.

'We'll go to the back of the cow pens,' he says. 'No one will see us there.'

'Dick!' I say. 'What *is* going on?'

But Dick just carries on pulling my hand. I find myself running alongside him to the cow pens.

Once we have settled down, behind the empty mangers where there's not so much dust, Dick says, 'It's important, Jill.' He tells me he was at the local shop with his mother this morning. 'It's just small,' he goes on. 'It's in the village and everyone gets their newspapers there.'

'What's this got to do with Jack?' I say. I scuff my shoes in the dirt. I like the way it makes a small cloud of dust.

'Because they were talking about someone and I think it was him.'

'Why?' I say. I'm listening now, staring at Dick.

'No one knew I was there. My mum was just parking the car and I'd gone in to get some sweets. All these women were looking at the front page of the newspaper and they were saying how the little boy had come to live round here.'

'What little boy?' I say. 'What are you talking about?'

'I'm not exactly sure,' he says. 'They were pointing at a picture and saying they wondered if he looked like that now. They were talking about some horrible thing that had happened. Then someone said the name Jack. There can only be one Jack who's come here recently and that's . . .'

'Jack,' I say. 'You think they were talking about my Jack?'

Dick nods fervently.

'Then, when my mum came into the shop, everyone went silent. When we got back in the car I was going to ask her about it, but she had a really bad look on her face, so I didn't.'

Dick and I sit in silence for a while. Then he gets up and starts drawing patterns in the dust with a piece of straw he found in the manger.

'Do you know any more than that?'

He gives me an honest sort of look.

'No,' he says. 'Do you?'

Then I tell him about the conversations I've heard between Uncle Paul and Auntie Glenda.

Dick sits back down. He sucks on the end of the straw.

'Something's going on, isn't it?' he says. 'And it's to do with Jack.'

I nod and feel as though I'm going to cry.

Suddenly Dick looks at me.

'Sorry about yesterday,' he says. 'I don't know why I got cross. I feel sorry for Jack. I want to help him.'

'So do I,' I say.

'It's just that it's . . . it's . . . odd, that he doesn't speak.'

'I know,' I say.

Dick and I sit a bit more.

Finally he gets up and says, 'Everyone's going out, right?'

I nod.

'Well then,' he says, 'it's time to look for clues.'

I don't say anything, so he comes over and kneels down.

'You in, Jill?' he asks.

'Yes,' I say. 'I'm in.'

Chapter Eight

Dick and I sit behind the mangers in the cow pens for at least half an hour until we see Auntie Glenda go off in Uncle Paul's van.

'She off to the market?' Dick asks.

I nod.

Then we wait for Uncle Paul and Jack to go and see the combine harvester. It takes them ages. Jack keeps on coming out of the house and chasing the chickens round the yard. Then, just as I think he's about to leave with Uncle Paul, he disappears back into the house again.

'Are they ever going to go?' Dick asks. He's sucking a piece of straw, turning it round and round in his mouth.

'I think so,' I say.

Eventually, Jack comes out followed by Uncle Paul. At one point they pass so near us, I can barely let myself breathe. I can hear Uncle Paul telling Jack all about the combine harvester.

'It's called a combine,' he is saying, 'because it *combines* many jobs in one. It cuts, threshes and harvests all at the same time. That's why it's so big.'

Jack tucks his hand into Uncle Paul's and looks at him with his eyes shining so brightly, it almost hurts me to see it. Part of me wants to stand up and say, 'Take me with you, Jack' because it looks like he is going to have such a good time. But Dick puts a hand on my arm and nods his head towards the house.

'Let's go,' he says.

We've been in the sitting room for ages now. We've looked everywhere: behind the curtains, in the dresser, even in the piano.

In the end, I plonk myself down on the sofa next to Mr Parker.

'I'm hot and tired,' I tell Dick who is still sifting through the books on the shelves. 'We've looked everywhere in this room and there's nothing. I don't even know what we're supposed to be looking for.'

Dick flops down next to me.

'Clues,' he says.

'Like what?' I ask him.

Dick furrows his brow. 'Well, those women in the shop were looking at a newspaper so . . . newspaper clues. Where would your aunt and uncle keep them?'

'I don't know,' I say. 'I've never seen them read a newspaper.'

'The kitchen? The pantry? You take the kitchen. I'll do the pantry.'

Half an hour later, we still haven't found anything and I'm beginning to think there's nothing to find.

I've gone through every drawer and cupboard. I've even checked the newspaper Auntie Glenda wraps the potatoes in. I asked Auntie Glenda once *why* she wrapped their potatoes in newspaper and she said it kept them fresh. I told her my mum kept potatoes in the fridge. Auntie Glenda looked at me for a bit and then said, 'Well, Jill, that's an odd place to keep them.' So I am thinking of odd places to keep things but, still, I find nothing.

Dick's been having a great time in the pantry. Every time he comes out to see how it is going in the kitchen, he has something stuffed in his mouth.

'Never knew fig rolls were so tasty,' he said the last time he came to see how I was doing. He had crumbs spluttering out of his mouth. I threw a tea towel at him.

But now we don't know what to do. We are sitting at the kitchen table drinking juice and finishing off the fig rolls. Mr Parker, the cat, has joined us and Dick sighs as he strokes Mr Parker's silken ears.

'I give up,' I say. I put my legs up on the table. 'I'm so tired and it's so hot.'

'We can't give up,' says Dick. 'There's got to be something . . .'

'Why has there got to be something?' I say to him. 'Maybe there isn't anything. Maybe those women in the shop were talking about someone else. Maybe . . .' I suddenly feel I'm going to cry. 'We shouldn't be doing this,' I say. 'I shouldn't be here with you. I should be out with Jack having a nice time with him and Uncle Paul. I've never seen a combine before and Jack's not used to being without me. He won't like it. He . . .'

'He looked like he was doing all right to me,' says Dick.

I get up. I want to hit him he's made me so angry.

'That's just mean,' I say. 'You can be quite horrible sometimes you know. You really hurt Jack yesterday and now you're picking on me and—'

But Dick isn't listening. He is staring at the kitchen door, looking towards the stairs.

'The attic!' he says. 'I knew it. There's an attic in this house, isn't there? There must be one because when I've looked up at your bedroom window I've seen those eaves above. Last year, wasps went in and out and I remember thinking there must have been a nest.'

'Thanks a lot for telling me!'

'*Last* year. Anyway, wasps aren't interested in us. They just go about their business. Now, how do you get in to the attic?'

'I don't know. Anyway, I'm not going in if there are wasps in there.'

'Jill, I've just told you . . .' Dick looks at the clock. 'Quick,' he says, 'we've got to go now. Your aunt could be home in about half an hour. That's when the market closes so . . .'

He gets up and starts going up the stairs.

'Come on,' he says.

At the top of the landing, we see the door. It's not a door really, more like a trap door in the ceiling.

'That's it!' says Dick excitedly. Then he carries on as if to himself, 'Now, how do they get up there. A stepladder?'

He gives me a quick look.

'Whose is this bedroom?' he says, pointing to Auntie Glenda's and Uncle Paul's room.

'We can't go in there,' I say quickly but Dick opens the door and disappears. I follow him reluctantly. I've never been in their bedroom before. It smells of old perfume. There's a small dressing table on one side of the room stacked full of bottles and pots. A pale blue nightdress trimmed with lace is laid out on the pillow. I am transfixed by it, then suddenly embarrassed. I shouldn't be looking at what Auntie Glenda wears in bed.

'Dick,' I say, 'we should get out of this room. It's not right.'

'Ha!' I hear him say. 'I knew it!'

He appears from out of the en suite bathroom with a small stepladder.

'It was behind the door,' he says. 'Evidence see?'

'Of what?'

'That someone goes into that attic.'

I sigh. I am beginning to feel really uncomfortable.

'I don't know,' I say. 'What if someone comes home? What if . . .'

But he is already out of the bedroom and climbing up the ladder.

There is hardly any light in the attic, just some chinks coming through gaps in the roof tiles where the sun blasts through like laser beams.

'There's boxes over there,' says Dick, wandering over to the gable end where there are more chinks of light. 'I think they're full of newspapers. Come and see.'

I go over, screwing my eyes up. There are about three cardboard boxes full of newspapers.

'Sit here,' says Dick, motioning towards a beam. He hands me a box. 'We better start reading then,' he says. 'There's a lot to get through.'

I pick up the first newspaper cutting. It says, 'The Prize for the Best Friesian Goes to Mr Paul Hartland' and above it is a picture of Uncle Paul and a big black and white cow. Uncle Paul is beaming at the camera.

'What's that about?' asks Dick.

'A cow winning Uncle Paul a prize. What are you reading about?'

'A bloody chicken with an egg-laying problem.'

'That's probably from *Poultry World*.'

'What?' says Dick, sounding amazed.

'I found a copy downstairs yesterday. I know all about Rhode Island Reds.'

'Just keep reading,' says Dick.

I work my way through the box. It turns out Uncle Paul's won loads of awards for his cows. He even got a special commendation for his Hereford bull.

I am about halfway through when Dick suddenly calls out.

'I've found something.' His voice is trembling.

'What?' I say. 'What have you found?'

'A cutting. More than one cutting. I'm not sure . . . I don't know . . .'

'What's it about?' I go towards where Dick is sitting.

'It's about a murder,' he says. 'It's about a few murders. Several women were found strangled in London. I can't see properly. It says they were all murdered in the space of a couple of years and their bodies were all found on – I can't read this bit. On . . . on . . . on . . . and there's a picture of a small boy.'

'Is it Jack?' I say quickly. My heart feels as if it's in my mouth.

'I don't know,' says Dick. 'His face has been made all fuzzy. There's a caption here. It reads – let me see. It says . . .'

Just then we hear a car pull up outside.

'Dick!' I say. 'Quick! Auntie Glenda's home. We've got to get out of here.'

'But I need to see what it says, Jill. I need to—'

'No!' I say and I start to pull him towards the trap door. 'We have to get out now!'

Somehow we manage to get out of the trap door and swing down. Dick gets the stepladder back in place just as Auntie Glenda comes through the front door laden with bags.

She stops dead when she sees us.

'What have you two been doing?' she asks us. She looks very suspicious.

'We've been playing,' says Dick.

'Yes,' I say. I can barely speak. My heart is beating so fast, I'm finding it hard to breathe normally.

I look at Dick. He has a cobweb in his hair and there's a streak of dust down his face. I'm hoping it's so dark at the top of the stairs and with Auntie Glenda just having come in from the light, she won't notice.

'I didn't know you were here, Dick,' she says.

'I came over to see Jill.'

'Help her collect the eggs, did you?'

I realise with a pang that I haven't actually collected the eggs yet.

'I've left the basket outside,' I say to Auntie Glenda. 'Can Dick and I go and get it?'

Auntie Glenda nods. She turns her back on us to go into the kitchen.

'You've a cobweb in your hair,' I whisper to Dick. He bends his head towards me. I am just about to get it out when Auntie Glenda re-appears.

'Once you've helped Jill with the eggs you should go home, Dick,' she says 'I saw your dad at the market and he says he needs you to work on the farm this afternoon. He says there's

71

another storm coming and he needs the animals moving.'

'All right,' says Dick.

We go outside and collect the eggs. They are warm and brown.

Neither of us speaks but then, as I place the final egg in the basket, Dick says, 'Why would your uncle have cut stuff out from the newspapers about a murder?'

I look to the skies. The storm clouds are gathering.

'I don't know,' I say. 'I really don't know.'

Chapter Nine

I am in bed again, watching Jack as his eyelids start to close. I think I spend too much of my time in bed. I think children are always asked to go to bed really early so the adults can get them out of the way. My mum always tells me that children need lots of sleep but she's always so tired, I think *she* needs lots of sleep. I can't tell her that because it would probably make her cross with me. She gets cross quite a lot, especially when I ask her questions. What she doesn't understand is that I *like* asking questions. I want to ask Uncle Paul and Auntie Glenda loads of questions. I can't because they told me and Jack to go to bed about an hour ago even though it was straight after tea and I told them I wasn't tired.

I think they are worried about us. Or, to be a bit more specific, me.

It all started after Dick left when I dropped three eggs as I went back to the house. I just took those eggs and on purpose let them fall from my hands and watched them as if they were in slow motion. They fell and broke open on the ground in front of the house. The yolks and whites spread everywhere, making a real mess and I didn't care.

Auntie Glenda watched me drop the eggs. She saw some of the sticky whites run onto the tips of my plimsolls. I could see her at the window, pursing her lips but, when I got in through the door, she didn't mention it. She just said, 'Go and change please, Jill.' So I went up to my bedroom and put on the brand new sandals my mum had packed for me.

Then I sat and looked out of the window, closed my eyes and tried to think back. I tried so hard my head hurt. I remembered the heat of a summer long gone. I must've been very young. I remember looking out of the window on to, what? Fields, I think. Something like that. I used to look out at night when it was dark and deep like the sea outside. I asked my mum about it once. 'What was out behind us when we lived in the flat before we lived here?' She looked jittery. 'I told you,' she said, 'it doesn't matter where we used to live. We live here now.'

I know Jack and I shared a room then. We've always shared a room. So I lay on my bed before tea and tried to make my mind work. It made it hurt so much I got a headache. Then, just as I was about to give up, I heard Uncle Paul talking outside and footsteps on the gravel.

'That was fun, Jack, wasn't it?' he was saying. 'It's an amazing thing, a combine. They used to do all that with a horse and cart years ago. Can you imagine?' Then I heard him say, 'Those clouds are back again. There's a big storm coming in, that's what the forecast said. I haven't seen two storms in a row like this since, well, since you were a small boy.'

I didn't look out of the window. I didn't want to see Jack looking as happy as I knew he was. I could *feel* his happiness coming straight through that window.

Later, at dinner no one was talking much at the table. Jack was eating, solidly munching a bit like one of the cows we saw the other day. He picked up his fork and put a bit of food in his mouth and then munched, munched, munched moving his mouth about in circles, smiling away to himself.

And then, suddenly, an evil thing came to me. I don't know why it did but it just popped into my head. Before I could stop it, I found myself telling Uncle Paul and Auntie Glenda what Dick had told me about the shop.

'Why were the women talking about Jack in the village shop?' I said. 'Dick told me they were saying something and it was about Jack and—'

Auntie Glenda, who had been clearing the plates, dropped her knife CLANG! on the floor. Jack looked up at me. I felt really bad because this pang of something flitted straight across his face. It was as though he'd seen a ghost. He looked right at me and he seemed all sad and scared. Then, quick as a flash, he'd gone back to eating again, only this time his head was bowed and he stared at nothing but his plate. He wouldn't look at me.

I felt really bad then.

I was about to get up and stroke his hair and say sorry but suddenly Auntie Glenda turned to me and said, 'It's time for bed now, Jill.'

'I don't want to go to bed,' I said.

'You said you had a headache,' Auntie Glenda continued. 'You came downstairs earlier and asked me for some headache pills, remember?'

'Yes,' I said, 'and now it's gone and I don't want to go to bed. I want to know—'

Suddenly, Uncle Paul stood up. He had a strange look on his face. I thought I was about to be in real trouble, but he just came towards me and took my arm really gently. He said, 'Go upstairs to bed, Jill. This storm that's coming is something you should just get away from. Go and sleep. It'll be good for both of you.' He motioned towards the stairs. I went up to bed with Jack following behind.

As I lie on my bed and shut my eyes, I can see these horrible little white dots zooming round my eyelids. Then I see Jack's face smiling at me. Then his mouth is turning wide and blood-red like a clown's. I want to scream but I can't because Jack's asleep. I can hear the rolling of the thunder and I don't want him to wake up and get scared again.

The next thing I know, I hear screaming. Terrible, terrible screaming as though someone's being tortured. At first, I think I am dreaming. I think I must still be having a nightmare. I think it must be Jack as a clown screaming in my head, but then I open my eyes and I see him. Jack. He is standing up on his bed staring out of the window and he is screaming and screaming. I can't really believe it is him making a noise. All I can see is the back of his head shaking, his arms outstretched and his hands scrabbling at the window like a cat trying to claw its way out. I leap up from my bed and run to him.

*

Jack's voice is going round and round in my head. I try to hold him but his screaming is piercing, piercing. For a moment I can't understand what is going on. I can't stop Jack from making this horrible noise. He is staring straight out of the window. His face has gone white and his mouth is wide open and he is screaming, 'No! No! No!' at the top of his voice. I throw my arms tightly round him and hug him hard.

'Jack!' I say. 'Stop! Jack! Jack! You are screaming. It's you and you are screaming.'

But he won't stop. He is shaking and staring. I look out to see what he is looking at, but it's dark and raining heavily and I can't see clearly. Jack has thrown the window wide open. The rain is splattering in as if we're on an open boat on the sea. It's soaking Jack's pyjamas. The thunder cracks above us. It rumbles loud and Jack is still screaming long and loud.

A flash of lightning shoots to the ground like a whip cracking. There, right in front of us, illuminated in black and white, is Uncle Paul. He is staring up at the window in shock, his eyes wide open, his mouth pulled back in a grimace. Rain is pouring off his cap and down his face. He has something with him but I can't see what it is. Another streak of lightning flashes up and I can make out he is dragging a large heavy sack behind him. Out of the open end flops the small perfect hooves and the head of the beautiful calf; its tongue lolling out.

Uncle Paul is plunged back in to darkness and Jack screams hysterically.

'I saw you!' he screams out of the window. 'I saw you! I saw you!'

He turns to me and looks panic-stricken; it's as though he is possessed by the devil. His eyes roll back in his head.

'I saw him!' he screams at me, high-pitched again. 'No! No! No! No!'

I can hear Uncle Paul shouting from outside, 'Jack! Jack! It's me. It's Uncle Paul.' Just as Auntie Glenda rushes in, crashing open the door, Jack falls down on to the bed in a silent faint.

I don't really know what happens next. It becomes a blur to me. All I can do is stare at Jack. He's totally still. He looks as if he's dead. Suddenly someone throws water over him and he starts to splutter. Uncle Paul is there and he has tears rolling from his eyes. He goes and grabs Jack in his strong arms and starts saying, 'It's OK, Jack. It's OK. It's me, your Uncle Paul. Your Uncle Paul.' Jack splutters some more. Uncle Paul holds some water to Jack's lips. His eyes open and he looks straight at Uncle Paul.

He is wild and sad, then he starts to cry and tears come out of his eyes. I go to him and take him in my arms too and I am crying, crying, crying along with him.

Chapter Ten

Uncle Paul, Auntie Glenda, me and Jack are sitting at the kitchen table. Jack is shivering even though, once he'd come round and stopped crying so much, Auntie Glenda gave him a hot bath and changed his pyjamas. I have a face as white as chalk. I know that because I was with Jack in the bathroom and I caught sight of myself in the mirror. I saw Uncle Paul staring at Jack from the bathroom door and his face was all contorted and his eyes were red.

I sat in the bathroom with Jack while he was in the bath. Auntie Glenda was speaking to him softly as she soaked his back.

'There, there, Jack,' she was saying. 'It's all right. Everything will be fine. Don't you worry now.'

I looked at his back and his long arms and legs. He's got brown, I thought, like a chicken's egg.

Jack just stared ahead of him though. He barely even moved. In fact, Jack hasn't spoken another word since he fell down on the bed and eventually stopped crying. He's silently drinking hot chocolate now, watching the dark streaks swirl round the milk.

I want to say something to him but I don't know what. I want him to speak to me again. I want to hear his voice but, somehow, I don't think he's going to.

'Jack,' I say, 'you talked.'

He doesn't look at me.

'You talked, Jack. You looked at me and you said words, but something happened didn't it? What was it? Can you tell me?'

I suddenly feel like crying again. What if Jack never speaks to me ever again? I don't think I could bear it.

I go over and take his hand.

'Please, Jack,' I say. 'Please speak to me about what happened to you. I want to hear your voice.'

But Jack just looks at me ever so sadly and shakes his head.

'Why?' I say. 'Why?'

'Because he can't,' says Uncle Paul roughly. 'He just can't.'

'Paul, please,' says Auntie Glenda. She sounds as if she is pleading with him.

'No, Glenda,' he says. 'It's time they knew. It can't remain a secret much longer anyway and it's best they hear it from us.'

82

'But their mother – I mean, is it our decision to make? I don't think it is.'

'No,' he says brusquely. 'Their mother has forfeited that right under these circumstances. Nothing has happened. No child psychologist, no speech therapist. No one has tried to help unlock this boy. Now even people in our local village are talking about him. I'm not blaming her. She's been through hell, but, if we don't tell him, that poor boy there will never speak again. Or he'll hear it from other people. That would be a disaster. I'm not going to let that happen.'

Auntie Glenda looks down. Mr Parker jumps on her lap.

'I don't know,' she says quietly.

'You told me you found her,' Uncle Paul motions to me, 'searching around with Dick! She's not stupid. Neither is Dick. She's going to find out soon and it'll be confusing and horrible for her. No, Glenda. This is the right thing to do. I'll settle it with their mother. I should've settled it a long time ago.'

Auntie Glenda nods her head silently and Uncle Paul turns to us.

'There's no easy way of saying this,' he says. 'It's something you need to know. The reason you don't see your dad, the reason you moved, the reason you are down here and we've got rid of the TV and get no newspapers from the shop is . . .' he sighs. 'Is that your father was convicted of murder a few years ago. Recently he appealed for the conviction to be overturned. That's why you are here, to stop you from being recognised.'

I stare at him. I can't take in what he is saying.

'I don't understand,' I say.

Auntie Glenda chips in.

'It's very hard,' she says. She reaches out a hand and takes mine in hers. 'I'm so sorry, Jill.'

'My father's a murderer?' I say. 'My father has killed other people and no one has ever told me and Jack this?'

'It was a difficult decision your mother took back then,' says Auntie Glenda. 'It's so complicated. No one knows why he did it. His appeal has just been turned down. Your mum will be coming to pick you up soon and she'll explain the rest.'

'No!' I say, suddenly angry. 'I don't get it. My father's a murderer. How can that be true? Who did he murder?'

'Women,' says Uncle Paul. 'Women he didn't know.'

'Why would he do that?' I say, tears streaming down my face.

'I don't know,' says Uncle Paul. 'There was a psychology report. Apparently he was suffering from intense stress, but no one knows really. There was some suggestion that he had a Jekyll and Hyde personality. I mean, Glenda and I would never have thought it.'

'But what's this got to do with Jack? Why would Jack's face be on the front of a newspaper? This doesn't make sense to me. He didn't try to kill us or Mum did he?'

'Oh no!' says Auntie Glenda. 'Oh, absolutely not. It was strangers, always strangers not . . . Oh God, no . . . Not his own family.'

'So why is Jack in the papers then?'

Uncle Paul sighs very heavily.

'OK, Jill,' he says. 'When you were small and Jack was even smaller, you lived in a flat backing onto Wanstead Flats in London.'

'I know,' I say. 'I keep having a memory of it, of fields or something. I've asked Mum about it, but she doesn't want to talk about it.'

'Yes, well, that's where she lived with you two and your dad. We didn't see you much then, just the occasional trip out. We took you to the river once. I was playing with you, trying to throw you in the water and you were having none of it.'

'That was you? I thought it was my dad.'

Uncle Paul shakes his head slowly.

'No. Your father wasn't around much. He

worked as a lorry driver and went all over the country. That's why he wasn't traced for a while. One night, the night your dad was caught, it was very stormy and . . . Well, the police think Jack saw your dad in the act of doing something . . . doing something bad.'

'Why?' I ask. 'Why does anyone think that?'

'Because your mum found Jack staring out of the window and screaming, just as he was tonight. A few minutes later, the police found your dad on the Flats loading a body into his car. It was a young girl. He had her wrapped up in a rubbish bag and . . . No one knows what Jack saw. No one has ever known what Jack saw. Apart from tonight, he's never spoken a word since. The police thought he must've seen his father with the body. It wasn't very well wrapped. It was all coming to an end for your dad anyway. I think he knew the police were on his trail and maybe he was panicking.

'Anyway, the police asked Jack what he'd seen, if he had seen a man with this poor girl on the night of the storm. He just nodded. He was asked to identify the man and he pointed straight to a picture of his dad. It never got used in court though. Jack was too young to give reliable evidence, you see. It got out in the press and was reported everywhere that somehow Jack had got your father – his own father – convicted, which is not true. Your mother decided to move you away, somewhere she thought no one would recognise you. She changed all your names to her mother's maiden name and hoped you wouldn't be identified, and you weren't. When the appeal started she was worried it would all get raked up again.'

I sit there. I can barely take any of this in. I stare at Uncle Paul.

'But why wouldn't Jack speak?'

Uncle Paul shrugs in a desperate way. 'Maybe because what he saw terrified him so much, he could never speak about it. It would've torn you apart to know, Jill. I think he didn't want to hurt you or hurt himself in the process but tonight . . . Tonight with the storm and him looking out of the window and me with that poor calf that had been struck by lightning falling out of the back of that sack – it must've brought it all back.' Uncle Paul shivers slightly. 'Poor boy,' he says. 'Poor, poor, Jack. I think that's why he spoke because it all came back to him.'

Auntie Glenda reaches out and takes Uncle Paul's hand. She nods her head gently at him.

I look at Jack and he looks at me.

'Is that why you bury things?' I ask him. 'Did you see Dad do that? Bury something?'

Jack doesn't move a muscle.

'Maybe he buries things to give them a proper send off,' says Auntie Glenda. 'Maybe that's his way of honouring the dead, to give them a good burial.' She shakes her head. 'I don't know,' she says. 'There's so much that boy knows, I fear he will never let it all out.'

'But he has to,' I say. 'You have to let it out, Jack,' I say to him. 'It's the only way. Uncle Paul's right. You have to talk about it. Tell me, tell me what happened to you because I love you, Jack. You've had such a horrible time and I love you. Don't you believe me?'

But Jack just keeps looking at me and doesn't say a thing.

EPILOGUE

Jack and I are going home now. Our mum came to pick us up. It was all such a flurry I barely got to say goodbye to anyone, only Uncle Paul and Auntie Glenda. That was weird because, when we left, I thought Auntie Glenda looked like she was going to cry.

'Goodbye, Jill,' she said, clutching at me. 'Goodbye, Jack.' Then she kissed me on my cheek and patted Jack on the arm. Uncle Paul came over and gave us both a big hug. I could smell him all earthy and damp.

'Take care of yourselves,' he said and his voice came out gruff and raspy.

He went to hug my mum but she pushed him away and I saw her look at him as though she was really furious.

'You had no right,' she said in this really low voice, but then she caught me listening to them so she stopped.

Uncle Paul just took her hand in his.

'It was the right thing to do,' he said to her. 'You'll see.'

Suddenly my mum bowed her head. Then she grabbed our hands and pulled us into the car.

The weather has changed. After the storm was over, the heat left as though it had been a visitor who was never meant to stay. Now the mornings are damp and the days colder.

Dick came round to see us the morning after the storm, but my Auntie Glenda wouldn't let him come in.

'They were up all night with that storm,' I heard her tell him. 'They're exhausted, Dick. Maybe tomorrow.'

I saw him look up at my window and I shrank back. I just didn't know what to say.

I think now I won't be able to say goodbye to him and that makes me sad. In a way, I want to tell him what's happened but it all seems so unreal. It's as if Uncle Paul has told me a story, a bad and horrible story, but a story, not something that is really true. I think if I told Dick, he'd understand. He wouldn't care my dad's a murderer. He'd just care about what happened to Jack. I told Auntie Glenda before I left that I wanted to see Dick but she told me there was no time.

'Write him a letter, Jill,' she said. 'I'll get it to him.'

As we drive out of the farm though, I see him. He is standing at the end of the lane, as if he is waiting for us. I want to say goodbye to him but my mum is in such a hurry, I don't dare ask her to stop. Instead, I just stare at him out of the window. Dick puts a hand up to me and I give him a little wave. I am about to tell Jack that Dick is hoping to say goodbye, but Jack is staring ahead so hard I think it might be better if I don't. I know Jack's probably upset with Dick. He doesn't know Dick wanted to apologise to him, but I'll tell Jack soon, when the time is right.

Now we are bowling along the motorway and the junctions are flashing past. Mum's humming a bit. She's happy because she doesn't need to look at a map now. She says she knows her way back to London.

Then she stops humming and looks at me in the rear-view mirror.

'Everything's going to change, Jill,' she says. 'It'll be better. I know . . . I know what's happened here and . . . Maybe your Uncle Paul was right. You probably did need to know, but I'm so sorry it wasn't me who told you. I should've done it. It's just that it's been so, so . . . and I didn't know how to.'

'It's all right, Mum,' I say. 'I understand.'

She flashes me a small smile.

'When we get home, I'll explain it all, in more detail than Uncle Paul has told you. I'll tell you everything you need to know. I've been to the social services. They say they'll help any way they can, a speech therapist for Jack, for example. I already met one while you were away and I've talked to a child psychologist. Your Uncle Paul thought that would be a start, you know.'

'That's really good, Mum,' I say.

'Shanice could come and play. We'll see people. We'll get a telly. We'll go places, see things. Everything will be better, Jill. Everything.'

As she's talking, I look at Jack. I don't listen to the words any more. I just want to be quiet with Jack. I look at him sitting with me in the back of the car, him and me, Jack and Jill. He looks back at me, his eyes all big and round and solemn. I reach out and touch his hand.

'Well,' I say, 'that was something, wasn't it?' All of a sudden, I think I'm going to cry. Then I look at Jack again and I give a big swallow because I don't want to upset him.

'You all right?' I say eventually.

Jack nods.

'Yeah,' he says in his little voice. 'I'm fine, Jill, just fine.'

Then he tucks his hand into mine and gives it a little squeeze.

Quick Reads 📖

Books in the Quick Reads series

Quick Reads 📖

Great stories, great writers, great entertainment

Quick Reads are brilliantly written short new books by bestselling authors and celebrities. Whether you're an avid reader who wants a quick fix or haven't picked up a book since school, sit back, relax and let Quick Reads inspire you.

We would like to thank all our partners in the Quick Reads project for their help and support:

Arts Council England
The Department for Business, Innovation and Skills
NIACE
unionlearn
National Book Tokens
The Reading Agency
National Literacy Trust
Welsh Books Council
Basic Skills Cymru, Welsh Assembly Government
The Big Plus Scotland
DELNI
NALA

Quick Reads would also like to thank the Department for Business, Innovation and Skills; Arts Council England and World Book Day for their sponsorship and NIACE for their outreach work.

Quick Reads is a World Book Day initiative.
www.quickreads.org.uk   www.worldbookday.com

Quick Reads

Great stories, great writers, great entertainment

Follow Me

Sheila O'Flanagan

Headline Review

The romantic tale of a career girl, a handsome stranger and chips

Pippa Jones is 20-something and single. She likes chips, country music and her cat. She also loves her career as number one sales rep for a computer firm. The only thing she hasn't got time for is men. Broken-hearted last time round, Pippa is sticking to girlfriends – and winning a dream trip to New York.

However, life isn't that simple. A rival firm is stealing her clients, and a tall, fair stranger is following her everywhere. He's in the bar, at dinner, even at her meetings. Is he a stalker? Whoever he is, he's about to turn Pippa's world upside down

Quick Reads

Great stories, great writers, great entertainment

Clouded Vision

Linwood Barclay

Orion

A chilling story of double-dealing, violence and murder

Ellie wakes covered in blood. She's trapped in a car, on a frozen lake. CRACK. The ice is breaking. One more crack and the car will plunge into the water below, taking Ellie with it …

Meet Keisha Ceylon – she's a nasty piece of work. She tricks families with visions she says will lead them to missing loved ones. However, one of those dodgy visions gets too close to the truth. Someone doesn't like it – and they're ready to kill to keep a terrible secret safe.

This chilling tale from bestselling writer Linwood Barclay will make your blood run cold.

Quick Reads 📖

Great stories, great writers, great entertainment

Strangers on the 16:02

Priya Basil

Black Swan

A very ordinary train journey goes horribly wrong

It's a hot, crowded train. Helen Summer is on her way to see her sister Jill and tell her an awful secret. Another passenger, Kerm, is on his way back from his grandfather's funeral. They are strangers, jammed against each other in a crowded carriage. Noisy school kids fill the train – and three of them are about to cause a whole heap of trouble. In the chaos, Helen and Kerm are thrown together in a way they never expected. Catching a train? Read *Strangers on the 16:02* and you'll never feel the same way about your fellow passengers again.

Quick Reads

Great stories, great writers, great entertainment

Men at Work

Mike Gayle

Hodder

A sweet, funny story about love and work

Ian Greening loves his job. He loves it so much he won't even take a promotion. He'd rather muck about with his workmates.

The other love of his life is girlfriend Emma. They've been together for years. The problems start when Emma loses her job and gets a new one in Ian's office. Ian doesn't like it at all. No more mucking about. No more flirting with the girls in admin. Ian wants her out. The question is, how? Can he do it without losing her or will it all end in tears?

Quick Reads

Great stories, great writers, great entertainment

Trouble on the Heath

Terry Jones

Accent Press

A comedy of Russian gangsters, town planners
and a dog called Dennis

Martin Thomas is not happy. The view he loves is about
to be blocked by an ugly building. He decides to take
action and organises a protest. Then things go badly
wrong and Martin finds himself running for his life. Along
the way he gets mixed up with depressed town
planners, violent gangsters and a kidnapped concert
pianist. Martin starts to wonder if objecting to the
building was such a good idea when he finds himself
upside down with a gun in his mouth.

This hilarious story from Monty Python star, Terry Jones,
will make you laugh out loud.

Quick Reads 📖

Great stories, great writers, great entertainment

Kung Fu Trip

Benjamin Zephaniah

Bloomsbury

A crazy martial arts adventure

From the moment Benjamin Zephaniah meets the 'kissy kissy' woman in his Chinese hotel, you know this isn't going to be an ordinary tourist story. Benjamin visits master Iron Breath to learn the secrets of Kung Fu – but it's not going to be easy, or cheap. Is he going to be ripped off? Would it be better to see Fat Thumb and his Smelly Finger? Why does everyone want him to sing like Eddy Grant? One thing's for sure, it's all a lot different to home.

Kung Fu Trip is a little bit daft and a whole lot of fun.

Quick Reads 📖

Great stories, great writers, great entertainment

Bloody Valentine

James Patterson

Arrow

This year Valentine's Day isn't for romance.
It's for murder

Mega-rich restaurant owner Jack Barnes and his second wife Zee are very much in love. However, their plans for Valentine's Day are about to be torn apart by the most violent murder. Who is the strange figure plotting this sick crime? Who hates Jack that much? There are plenty of suspects living in Jack's fancy block of flats. Is it them, or could it be the work of an outsider with a twisted mind? One thing's for sure, the police have got their work cut out solving this bloody mess.

This gory murder mystery will make you feel weak at the knees.

Other resources

Enjoy this book? Find out about all the others from **www.quickreads.org.uk**

Free courses are available for anyone who wants to develop their skills. You can attend the courses in your local area. If you'd like to find out more, phone 0800 66 0800.

 Don't get by get on 0800 66 0800

For more information on developing your basic skills in Scotland, call The Big Plus free on 0808 100 1080 or visit www.thebigplus.com

Join the Reading Agency's Six Book Challenge at www.sixbookchallenge.org.uk

read
readingagency.org.uk

Publishers Barrington Stoke (www.barringtonstoke.co.uk) and New Island (www.newisland.ie) also provide books for new readers.

 Barrington Stoke   OPEN DOOR

The BBC runs an adult basic skills campaign. See www.bbc.co.uk/raw.

BBC
raw
skills for everyday life

www.worldbookday.com